BUT MARTIN!

June Counsel

Illustrated by
Neal Layton

Picture Corgi

That first morning back at school

But that was before they found . . .

Lloyd's face was
round and brown

Lee's face
was smooth
and golden

Billy's face was square and red

and Angela's face was long and white

But Martin's face was . . .

Lee's hair was black and silky

Lloyd's
hair
was
black
and
bouncy

Billy's hair was red and spiky

and Angela's hair was fair and floaty

But Martin's hair . . .

Billy whistled

and Angela gasped

But Martin . . .

Then they began to play.

Lee skipped

Lloyd jumped

Billy chased

and Angela cartwheeled

But Martin . . .

When they got to the classroom
     Lee
       Lloyd
         Billy
           and
             Angela
              came
               through
                the door

But Martin came through the . . .

Now, Lee knew a little
Lloyd knew a lot
Billy knew a bit
and Angela knew most things
(so she thought)

But Martin knew . . .

When they had maths
Lee did take-aways
Lloyd did adds
Billy did matching
and Angela did take-away-you-can'ts!

But Martin did . . . .

the ANSWERS in HIS head!

And he showed them what to do . . .

and they all got it right!

When they had painting

Lee painted
her favourite
restaurant

Lloyd
painted the
winning goal

Billy painted a three-legged race

and Angela drew her family cat

But Martin painted . . .

HIS HOUSE ON MARS!
SPACE PORT
COOL!
PLANET EARTH 96MK
WELCOME TO MARS!

When school ended

Lee went home in her mum's new car
Lloyd went home on his battered old bike

Billy went home on the three-thirty bus
and Angela walked home on her own two feet

But Martin went home in his . . .